So Not the Drama!

By Acton Figueroa
Based on the series created by
Bob Schooley and Mark McCorkle

New York

Printed in the United States of America

First Edition
1 3 5 7 9 10 8 6 4 2

Library of Congress Catalog Card Number: 2004114360

ISBN 0-7868-4690-9

For more Disney Press fun, visit www.disneybooks.com
Visit DisneyChannel.com

BANK HEIST

"**C**an it be true?" Ron Stoppable yells from his friend Kim Possible's living room, where he's playing video games with her twin brothers. "Am I going to make it to Level 7? Am I really that good? YES!"

Kim Possible rolls her eyes as she stands at the kitchen counter making her first nonfat mochaccino of the day. Wow, he is just way too enthusiastic about video games, Kim thinks. I can't believe he actually got up early to come here and play against the Tweebs.

"Ron—" Kim begins as her Kimmunicator beeps. She looks at the screen. Her computer-genius friend Wade appears, his face partially covered by a breakfast sandwich.

"Hey, Kim," Wade says. "It looks like you're going to be busy this morning. Wait until you

Turn to the next page.

hear what your enemies have cooked up."

"What's the sitch, Wade? Can it wait until I finish my mochaccino?" asks Kim.

"I don't think so, Kim," replies Wade. "Not unless you want to see every last dollar in the world go right into your enemies' pockets."

Kim gulps her drink. "I'm listening, Wade."

"Okay, it seems there's a little trouble at the four largest Global Bank branches. Aviarius, Falsetto Jones, Frugal Lucre, and White Stripe are working together on a little—make that big—bank heist. And it's going to happen this morning!"

From the other room, Kim can hear Ron and the Tweebs arguing over who gets to play next. "Hold on a minute, Wade," says Kim. "Ron, come in here. We've got a job to do."

Ron dashes into the kitchen with his pet mole rat, Rufus. "Sounds excellent, Kim! What's up?"

Wade tells Kim and Ron the villains' plan. Four of Kim's most devious

Go to the next page.

archenemies are set to rob the four largest branches of Global Bank. If their plan works, they will take control of the money in everyone's bank accounts. "And you know what that means, Kim?"

"You bet, Wade," Kim replies. "No more shopping sprees at Club Banana for me—or anyone else! Ron, let's go!"

Kim and Ron are ready to stop the bad guys. Now it's up to *you*. Turn to the next page to help Kim decide which villain to go after first.

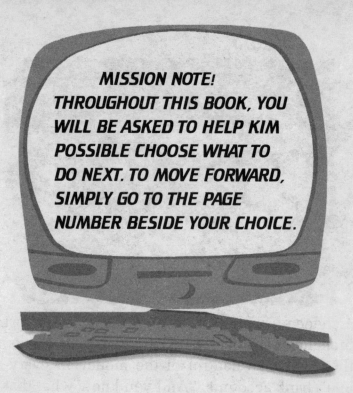

MISSION NOTE!
THROUGHOUT THIS BOOK, YOU
WILL BE ASKED TO HELP KIM
POSSIBLE CHOOSE WHAT TO
DO NEXT. TO MOVE FORWARD,
SIMPLY GO TO THE PAGE
NUMBER BESIDE YOUR CHOICE.

Which of Kim's archenemies should she go after? It's time for *you* to help Kim pick a villain!

 To pick Falsetto Jones, turn to page 15.

 To pick Frugal Lucre, turn to page 27.

 To pick Aviarius, turn to page 59.

 To pick White Stripe, turn to page 75.

Hey, there! Wade here! I'm checking in to remind you not to read this book like you normally would. Do not turn to the next page. Go back to page 6 and pick a villain for Kim and her friends to battle, then flip to the page number beside your choice and begin to read. As you read, you will be asked to make choices for Kim and her friends. These choices will send you to different pages all over the book. What happens to Kim and her friends will depend on your choices. If you come to a dead end, don't get tweaked. Just keep starting the book until you have helped Kim defeat all of the villains! There are tons of different endings, so you can read this book over and over and it will always be different. Ready? Okay, time to pick a villain!

"**B**oo-ya," Ron yells. "Nobody messes with the Nacho." Rufus peeps out of Ron's pocket and gives him a high five. Ron ties White Stripe up while Kim calls Wade on the Kimmunicator.

Wade e-mails the police. Kim picks up the bags of money and walks over to White Stripe, who is just waking up.

"So, White Stripe," Kim says to the groggy villain, "looks like your show just got canceled. Why were you wearing a Bueno Nacho uniform, anyway?"

"I worked there," White Stripe replied. "But I needed some cash fast for my new show."

"Hey, Kim!" Ron says. "He could do a reality show from prison!"

White Stripe sits up. "That's a brilliant idea! I'll use my phone call at jail to call my agent!"

Kim shakes her head as she and Ron leave to return the bags of money to Global Bank.

👍 You win! If you have captured all the villains, turn to page 52.

👍 To pick a new villain, turn to page 6.

"**R**on, go shut the door of the safe to lock them in," Kim says. "I'll stay by the front door to block them in case anything goes wrong. Okay?"

"Okay, Kim," whispers Ron. "I'm going in. Cover me!" Ron jumps up and sprints to the safe. Just as he reaches the heavy metal door, the chamster leaps up and clamps onto his shirt. "RRRRRR!" it growls. Rufus pops out of Ron's pocket and growls back.

Ron twirls around, trying to shake the little mutant off.

Ron spins a little harder. The chamster loses its grip and goes flying toward its master, who squeals, "My baby!" He catches the chamster and holds it close.

The bodyguards glare at Ron. Should he run to get Kim or stay and fight on his own?

☻ **To stay and fight, turn to page 11.**

☻ **To run and get Kim, turn to page 26.**

Kim climbs up the beams of the tower. As she gets closer to her birdbrained foe, she hears him talking to himself. "I'm rich! I'm the richest supervillain in the world!"

Kim turns around so she's facing away from the wall. Hanging by her hands, Kim positions her ejector-net sneakers so that the soles are facing the nest.

She counts to three and activates the little 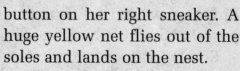 button on her right sneaker. A huge yellow net flies out of the soles and lands on the nest.

Aviarius stands up. "Kim Possible! I should have known," he says.

"That's right, Aviarius," says Kim. "Looks like your flight plan has been rejected. Time for me to return that money to Global Bank!"

👍 **You win! If you have stopped all the villains, turn to page 52.**

👍 **To pick another villain, turn to page 6.**

*R*ufus is way mad at the chamster for going after Ron. He jumps onto the floor, scurries up Falsetto, and punches the chamster's snout.

"OOOOOWWW!" squeaks the chamster.

Ron pops Falsetto in the jaw. Falsetto decides to fight. He kicks Ron in the knee. Ron hops around in pain. The bodyguards separate Rufus and the chamster.

Falsetto says, "Well, Stoppable, I guess you are stoppable, after all. We've got our money now, so we're leaving. Too bad your red-haired friend doesn't know about the secret exit at the back of the bank. Toodle-oo!" Falsetto steps out of the safe and slams the door.

Ron and Rufus are locked in the safe, and Falsetto escapes with the money.

👎 You lose—Falsetto's safe. To battle him again, turn to page 15.

Ron and Kim enter the courtyard facing Notre Dame, but it's so crowded they can hardly move.

"What's going on, Kim? These crowds are bigger than the ones at Smarty Mart on Dollar Day!" Ron huffs.

She pushes her way through the police barricade. "What's the sitch—I mean, what's the problem, officer?" she asks.

"Mademoiselle," the policeman says, "we have a big bird problem. You see that?" He points to a large pile of sticks on the ground. "A giant bird seems to have—how you say?—rejected these sticks for its nest, which is in the tower. Since sticks are falling on tourists, we've had to rope off some sections of the cathedral."

Kim spies a woman sitting on a bench with a bandage on her head. Should she talk to the woman or investigate the tower?

🌐 To investigate the tower, turn to page 65.

🌐 To talk to the woman, turn to page 79.

Kim starts to fall, but notices a piece of wood sticking out behind the letter. She grabs onto it and pulls her way back up to the platform. She leaps in front of White Stripe. "I'm not done with you yet, you stinker!" says Kim.

Pow! Pow! Kim throws hard punches. White Stripe punches her in the arm. "Ow!" yelps Kim. They trade punches and kicks and move closer and closer to the edge of the letter until Kim is cornered.

Just then, a huffing and puffing Ron heaves himself up onto the platform. He's carrying White Stripe's Bueno Nacho uniform. Ron plants himself in front of the villain and says, "You're a disgrace to this uniform, *mister*!" With just one punch, Ron knocks White Stripe out cold.

🌐 **Turn to page 8.**

As they go up the steps, Wade says, "The signal is getting stronger." At the top of the stairs is a gigantic door with the letters *FJ*. It's open, so they tiptoe in. It's Falsetto's bedroom.

"Wow!" whispers Kim. "He's got more beauty products than I do!"

"Kim, look over there." Ron points to a basket by the bed. A litter of chamsters is sleeping. "If we wake them up, their barking will alert Falsetto!" Kim motions to Ron to keep moving. They slip past the chamsters and onto the terrace.

"Kim, the signal is even stronger here," says Wade. "Keep moving in the same direction."

"But there's nowhere to go," says Kim, "unless we go up to the roof."

🌐 **Turn to page 36.**

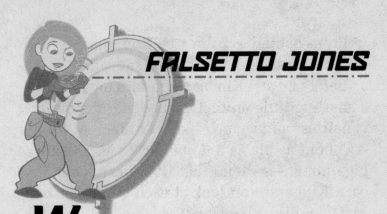

"**W**ade, can you say that again?" Kim says into the Kimmunicator. "I heard you, but I can't believe it!"

"Sure," says Wade. "Falsetto Jones has created a new breed of dog so small you can carry it in your shirt pocket. It's part Chihuahua, part hamster. He calls it a chamster."

It turns out that Falsetto Jones is en route to the New York City branch of Global Bank. Kim and Ron decide to go there and sneak inside. That way they can wait for Falsetto Jones and ambush him.

Once they're at the bank, Kim and Ron look for a good place to hide. The high ceilings and enormous waiting area are going to make it hard to stay out of sight. Luckily, the bank doesn't open for another hour, so no one is around.

Turn to the next page.

From behind a palm tree Ron hears a high-pitched noise—part bark, part squeal.

Before he and Kim can slip into the shadows, a snarling little animal dashes into the bank. It is hairless and shaped like a Chihuahua, except it's about as big as a doughnut hole. Its bark is big, though—so loud that Kim has to cover her ears. Kim and Ron look at each other questioningly. Is this a chamster?

Falsetto Jones runs into the bank, followed by two massive bodyguards. "Hey, Boss," rumbles one of them, "look who's here."

"So, Kim Possible," squeaks Falsetto Jones, in a voice so high-pitched that the chamster instantly stops barking. "Did you think you could stop me? Think again. I'm on a mission to bring my new breed of dog to the fashionable people of the world. People like me, who can never have too many beautiful things."

The body-

Go to the next page.

guards, as well trained as Falsetto's dog, break into applause.

"Tie them up!" squeals Falsetto, pointing to Ron and Kim.

Kim throws a punch at one bodyguard, but his stomach is like steel. They grapple. Kim gets three solid chops to his thick neck, but soon she is tied up alongside Ron. Falsetto and the bodyguards go to the vault and begin piling money into designer suitcases.

"Maybe Rufus could chew his way through the ropes," Ron says. Rufus pops out of Ron's pocket and smiles, baring his front teeth.

"Excellent idea, Ron!" says Kim. Rufus goes to work and soon they are free. Should they sneak up on Falsetto and the bodyguards or just slam the safe door shut?

⊕ To close the safe, turn to page 9.

⊕ To go fight, turn to page 71.

*O*n the count of three, Kim puts her jetpack backpack into gear and zooms up toward the nest. Above her she hears Aviarius chirp, "What's that noise?" Kim jets to him and pops him in the beak—*pow*!

"Ouch!" whines Aviarius. He hops up and snaps one of his wings at Kim, knocking her into the wall.

"Oof!" Kim hovers for a second, catching her breath. Then she kicks off from the wall and jets toward Aviarius, ready to uppercut the pesky bird. She gets closer and throws a punch. Aviarius ducks, and Kim misses completely. The momentum sends her straight into a beam.

Uh-oh! Kim's jetpack motor starts to sputter. She grabs onto one of the beams just below.

"Don't bank on catching me anytime soon," Aviarius calls as he gathers his money and flies away.

👎 **Aviarius flew the coop—** **you lose. To try to catch him again, turn to page 59.**

Kim steers in through the open window. Her motor chugs to a halt as they land in the dark tower. Ron feels along the wall with his fingers. "Hey, Kim," he says, "ready to light it up?"

"Okay, Ron, hold on." Kim finds her glitter pen/searchlight and turns it on.

"Wow! This place is so old!" Ron whispers.

"Look for signs of Aviarius. He's got to be here." Kim looks all around her. No feathers, no eggs, no bird droppings. Hmm . . .

Kim sees a small door along one wall and motions for Ron to follow her. They slip into the room and—*whoosh*—a rushing noise makes them spin around.

It's Aviarius's giant condor! His enormous wing is blocking the door. Kim and Ron are trapped until it flies away!

☞ **You lose. But don't get tweaked. Turn to page 59 to play again.**

Kim decides to help the woman. They walk over to the dressing room.

The old lady tries on the pants. The capris totally work on her.

"Dear," the old lady calls, "can you bring me one of those sequin shirts?" Kim steps into the dressing room with the shirt.

SLAM! The outer door to the dressing room swings shut. From the other side a voice yells, "I've got you now, Kim Possible! There's no way out!" Frugal Lucre pauses. "At least until Maya the dressing room attendant comes back from lunch. But I will have gotten all of the money by then. Ha-ha-ha!"

👎 **You're trapped. To try to outsmart Frugal Lucre again, turn to page 27.**

When Kim gets to the hair-care aisle, she sees the biker. He's wearing lots of leather and a chain-link bracelet. And he's bigger than Kim and Ron put together.

The biker sees them staring and puts down the jumbo-size hair gel he's looking at. "Hey . . ." he rumbles and points at them.

Ron jumps back.

"Hey, you . . ." the biker says. "What do you use on your hair? It looks real nice."

Ron steps out from behind Kim. "Me? Well, I use a little shampoo, although sometimes if I'm in a hurry . . ."

The biker pokes his meaty finger at Ron's chest and Ron flies back about three feet. Rufus sticks his head out and chatters angrily.

"I'm talking to you, little lady," the biker says, as he turns to Kim. "Your hair is real pretty. What do you use?" he asks.

🌐 **Turn to page 37.**

Kim and Ron follow the chips down Santa Monica Boulevard. The trail suddenly ends with a poodle nibbling the last chip.

"Looks like the dog ate the rest of the trail," Ron says. Rufus pops out of Ron's pocket and shakes his finger at the poodle.

"Now what are we going to do?" Ron asks. "Wait, I have an idea—the Bueno Nacho Hot Hot Hotline!" He whips out his cell phone and begins dialing. Meanwhile, Kim calls Wade who tells her that a small bank near the beach just received the largest online banking deposit ever! "That could be the work of White Stripe," says Kim. "I think that we should investigate."

But Ron has another idea. "Kim, there's a Bueno Nacho right around the corner. I think White Stripe might be there. Plus, I can get a burrito. Mmmmm!" Should Kim go to Bueno Nacho or go to the bank?

🌐 To go to the bank by the beach, turn to page 45.

🌐 To go to Bueno Nacho, turn to page 67.

"**I** still think we should have gone to Bueno Nacho, Kim," Ron says as they jog to the bank. "Even if White Stripe isn't there, we could have had a little lunch. I'm starving!"

"Ron! Would you forget about your stomach for a while?" Kim replies as they stop in front of the bank. Unfortunately, it's closed.

Kim thinks about the evidence. They know White Stripe is definitely the bank robber. They also know he's been wearing a Bueno Nacho uniform. So, if White Stripe isn't at the bank, he might be at Bueno Nacho.

"Okay, Ron, let's go to the Nacho," Kim says with a sigh.

"Bon diggity!" Ron replies with a smile.

🌐 **Turn to page 67 to go to Bueno Nacho.**

Kim decides to follow Bonnie, but accidentally knocks over a pile of hats.

Kim gives up on hiding. "Hi, Bonnie. How's your shopping going?"

"Oh, you think I'm buying these?" she says, pointing to the girlie T-shirts in her hand. "No, I was just looking for a present for my brother."

"The boys' rack is over there," Kim says, pointing to the other side of the store.

"Oh, uh, yeah," Bonnie says as she puts the shirts back on the rack. She goes to the boys' rack and pulls a shirt off. "He'll like this one. Or not." She turns to leave.

"Hey, Bonnie, wait!" Kim doesn't know what to say. She's got to stop Bonnie. "Did you hear about the Global Bank card thing? If you're the hundredth customer you get a free shopping spree."

Bonnie laughs. "Like I want a shopping spree here, Kim. I'll pay cash. Anyway, I really don't have time to talk." Bonnie turns to leave.

Kim scowls at her and thinks, Well, at least I don't shop at Smarty Mart.

🌐 **Turn to page 68.**

Kim jumps up onto the belt of the Salsa Parade. She crashes into Ron, who has been riding the Salsa Parade around and around, double dipping chips the whole time.

Ron loses his balance and kicks a bowl of salsa as he falls off the belt. The salsa lands on White Stripe, who is standing nearby.

"Ron! Grab White Stripe!" Kim yells from the conveyor belt. Ron makes a dive for White Stripe but can't get a grip. Salsa is slippery!

Kim jumps down off the Salsa Parade and moves in on White Stripe. "This is it, White Stripe! Why don't you just give up?" says Kim.

White Stripe backs up slowly. "I'll give up when I'm ready, Kim Possible," he says. "And I'M NOT READY!"

White Stripe jumps up onto the Salsa Parade and rides the conveyor belt into the kitchen. Kim and Ron follow him.

⊕ **Turn to page 64.**

Ron runs to the front door, but Kim's not there. He hides behind a pillar and looks around.

He spots Kim, but she's trapped by four of Falsetto's dogs. They look like the wolfhounds from the dog show where Kim and Ron first defeated Falsetto. Two of the dogs go after Ron. He skids around a desk and picks up speed as he runs down the center of the room.

As Ron turns the corner, he looks back. Kim is still trapped. The dogs are nipping at his heels. Just as they're ready to pounce, Falsetto calls out, "Heel!" The dogs stop. Falsetto ties Kim and Ron up again.

"We're leaving now— with the money!" Falsetto says with a smile as he turns and leaves.

👎 **You got dogged. No big. To fight Falsetto again, turn to page 15.**

FRUGAL LUCRE

"Okay, Wade, we're in front of Smarty Mart. You better tell me the sitch before we go in," says Kim. "I don't really want to be seen here."

"Hey, Kim," crackles Wade over the Kimmunicator. "It's like this. Frugal Lucre is way angry at Global Bank 'cause they charge such high checking fees. You know this guy has bigger problems than that, right? He lives with his mom and he's, like, thirty or something!"

"Let's not forget that he also works at Smarty Mart, Wade. That's enough to make anyone consider a life of crime," says Kim.

It turns out Frugal Lucre has set up the Smarty Mart computers with special hacking software. Every time a Global Bank customer buys something with their debit card, the software gets one step closer to cracking the bank's

Turn to the next page.

security code. When the hundredth person buys something at Smarty Mart—bingo!—all the money in Global Bank goes directly to that person's checking account.

Kim thinks for a second and says, "So then all Frugal Lucre has to do is figure out that person's account number so he can divert the money to his own account? But  how does he know that one hundred Global Bank card members will shop here today?"

"Hey, Kim!" shouts Ron, who's waving a Smarty Mart flyer. "Check this out! The hundredth Global Bank customer to use their debit card today gets a free five-minute shopping spree! It's gotta be me, Kim! It's just GOTTA!"

Kim says to Wade, "Forget I asked, Wade."

Kim has to find the Global Bank customers and either stop them from shopping or get them to pay cash.

"Okay, Kim, I hacked into the security cameras and the sales records for the day so far and

28

Go to the next page.

I've got good news and bad news." He pauses. "Well actually, I've got okay news and bad news. Err, well, whatever. It's like this," stammers Wade.

The okay news is that ninety-seven Global Bank shoppers have already used their cards. That means only three more cardholders need to make a purchase before the money transfers. The bad news is that one of three cardholders shopping now is Bonnie, Kim's cheerleading rival.

Kim gasps. "Bonnie? What is she doing at Smarty Mart? And who are the other two?"

Wade says, "An old lady and a biker dude."

It's time for you to help. Who should Kim go after first: the biker, the old lady, or Bonnie?

🌐 To go after the biker, turn to page 21.

🌐 To go after Bonnie, turn to page 56.

🌐 To go after the old lady, turn to page 70.

Kim whips her combination hair scrunchie/lariat off her ponytail and slips on a squashed juice box. Ouch! Kim goes down, and the lariat falls into a puddle of juice. Kim retrieves it and throws it—but it plops onto the floor. The juice seems to have affected the elasticity.

She looks up. Where is Frugal Lucre? She looks up and down the aisle. No sign of him.

Kim peeks in a freezer. As she does, Frugal Lucre sneaks up and pushes her right into a pile of reduced-fat chimichangas.

Just then, an announcement comes over the store's loudspeaker. "Attention, customers. The hundredth Global Bank customer has just checked out. We have a winner."

Frugal Lucre smirks at Kim, who's still buried in Mexican food. "Enjoy your lunch, Kim Possible!" he cries and runs away.

👎 **You got buried. To try again, turn to page 27.**

*K*im and Ron creep around the kitchen quietly, hoping for a sign—or a whiff—of White Stripe. The steam from the dishwasher makes it hard to see.

"Hey, Kim," whispers Ron. "Do you think he's left the kitchen?"

"I don't know, Ron, but it's really hot in here. On three, let's jump up and see if we can't scare him out. Ready? One, two, three!"

Kim and Ron jump up and—*wham!*—a blast of icy cold water hits them. They turn and see White Stripe holding the spray attachment of the dishwasher.

"Well, well, Kim Possible," White Stripe says with a laugh. "Looks like you're about to get hosed." White Stripe points to the hose behind them. Cold water hits the hot grill and sizzles, sending even more steam into the air.

Kim can't see a thing. Where is White Stripe?

⊕ **Turn to page 64.**

"**P**ut up your dukes, Frugal Lucre, and fight like a supervillain!" yells Kim Possible.

Frugal Lucre jumps out and gets in a boxing stance. "Bring it on, I'm ready to rumble." As Kim approaches him, Frugal Lucre gets a panicked look. He turns and runs away.

Kim dashes after him. She sees Ron up ahead, making bouncy balls from free hair gel. The pile of balls is at least two feet high and one ball is at least a foot tall. Rufus is busy chasing a ball back and forth across the aisle.

Hmm, Kim thinks. If you take one clumsy supervillain and add a lot of bouncy little balls, what do you get? She decides to find out.

"Hey, Ron!" shouts Kim. "Do you want to do a little bowling?"

Ron takes the giant ball, backs up, and bowls it right at his pile. Bouncy balls go everywhere.

"Hey! What gives?" yells Frugal Lucre as he tries to step around them. It's no use. He steps on one and—*crash!!*—down he goes.

"Steee—rrrike!" shouts Ron. "I win!"

Before Frugal Lucre can get up, the store

manager comes over. He looks down at Frugal Lucre and says, "You're fired! I can't have an assistant manager playing in the aisles like a little kid. Get out—now!"

Ron and Kim giggle. That's one less supervillain to worry about. With no access to Smarty Mart computers, he won't be able to get his money.

On the way out, Kim buys some Wacky Packy chewing gum and swipes her Global Bank card through the machine. Bells begin to ring and the manager snaps her picture.

"Congratulations, miss!" he says. "You're the one hundredth Global Bank customer! Tomorrow your picture will be in every newspaper in town!"

"You'll be the most famous Smarty Mart customer ever!" says Ron.

"Oh, great," Kim says with a groan.

👍 **You win! If you have stopped all the villains, turn to page 52.**

👍 **To pick another villain, turn to page 6.**

"I'm not sure those pants are going to look right. They're too . . ." Kim struggles to think of what to say. If the woman buys them, she could be the hundredth customer of the day.

"They're TOO perfect! That's what they are!" booms Frugal Lucre. He skips over to the old lady. You are a total *star* in those, ma'am." Frugal Lucre pauses, giving Kim a dirty look.

"Plus, I'll knock another ten percent off."

"Oh, I will buy them, then," says the old lady.

Frugal Lucre takes her arm. "I'll escort you to the cashier myself." He turns and glares at Kim.

There's nothing for Kim to do. The lady buys the jeans and wins a shopping spree. In all the excitement, Frugal Lucre slips out a side door and escapes. The money is as good as gone.

☞ **Frugal Lucre cashed out—you lose. Turn to page 27 to play again.**

"**S**o," Kim asks the biker, "are you going to buy the gel? It looks *really* nice." Kim is nervous. What if one of the other customers has bought something?

"I think I'll just use the free stuff every morning like your little friend said." The biker looks over at Ron.

The biker finishes fixing his hair. "Well, I'll see you 'round."

"Later, bro," says Ron, in a lame attempt to be biker-dude cool.

Wade's voice comes over the Kimmunicator. "Kim," he says, "it's too late. A report just came over the wire about Frugal Lucre's robbery."

☞ **You lose. To try to catch Frugal Lucre again, turn to page 27.**

*O*n the roof, Wade says, "The signal is way strong up here. Keep looking!" Ron and Kim peek around the potted shrubs and statues that are part of the roof garden. The Brooklyn Bridge looks almost close enough to touch.

Crash. Ron trips over a potted plant. They hear barking downstairs.

Kim looks around. They can go down the fire escape, or Kim can use her grappling hook to swing over to the Brooklyn Bridge.

What should they do?

🌐 **To swing onto the Brooklyn Bridge, turn to page 40.**

🌐 **To go down the fire escape, turn to page 53.**

Kim scans the shelves for her favorite hair gel. "Hey!" she exclaims. "They do have it! And look how cheap it is!"

"Why buy that?" Ron asks. "They've got free samples right here. If I used this hair gel, *which I don't*," he says, "I'd just come in here every morning for a free sample."

The biker takes some free gel and puts it in his hair. "How do I look?" he asks Kim.

"Great!" she says. "Just like the guy on TV."

Meanwhile, Ron has discovered that the hair gel bounces when it hardens. He starts to make a little pile of bouncy balls.

Should Kim stay or look for another customer?

⊕ **To stay with the biker, turn to page 35.**

⊕ **To find Bonnie, turn to page 56.**

⊕ **To look for the old lady, turn to page 70.**

"**R**on, we'll never get to the top if we wait on this line," says Kim. "It'll take all day!"

"Relax, Kim! It's moving just fine," Ron says.

Kim doesn't want to wait. "C'mon, Ron!" says Kim. "We're going up!" They tip-toe by the security guard to the basement room where all the elevator cables connect to the floor.

Kim pulls her combination hair grip/cable clamp from her pack and attaches it to her friendship bracelet—and voilà! Instant top-of-the-tower access, as long as Ron can hold on. Kim snaps the clamp onto the cable, Ron grabs onto her, and as the elevator whooshes up, so do they.

As they rise, they see the city of Paris all around them. Rufus sticks his head out of Ron's pocket and sighs.

"I know, ooh la la, right, Rufus?" Kim asks.

🌐 **Turn to page 44.**

Kim and Ron creep down the hallway. Ron stops at one of the doors. "Hey, Kim," he whispers, "check it out! That screen has to be, like, six feet wide!"

They enter the room. The far wall is filled with an enormous TV and shelves of DVDs. Ron can't believe his eyes.

"Woo-chow! I know Falsetto is a bad guy and all, Kim, but he sure has good taste in TVs. This thing is . . . yow!!!!"

While Ron is talking, three of Falsetto's henchmen creep out from behind the door.

"Uh-oh, Ron," says Kim. "Looks like we took a wrong turn." Rufus covers his eyes.

Kim strikes a fighting pose, but the tall bodyguard just smirks. "Unluckily for you," he says, "Falsetto likes complete darkness when he watches movies, so there are no windows in this room. The door, which is a superthick steel model, is the only way out. Oh, well." He slams the door shut and a key turns in the lock.

Kim, Ron, and Rufus are trapped.

👎 **You got slammed. To try again, turn to page 15.**

Kim throws her grappling hook at the Brooklyn Bridge.

"Um, K.P.," Ron says, "please tell me that you're not thinking of swinging us over there. If we fall, it's gonna be one big SPLAT."

"Just hang on, Ron," Kim instructs. Reluctantly, Ron grabs onto Kim as she swings Tarzan-style toward the bridge.

"AAAAAAAAA!!!" Ron cries. But Kim lands smoothly on the bridge. Ron lets go and tries to stand tall. "Just as I suspected, Kim," he says. "It was an easy, painless maneuver."

Kim rolls her eyes. "Let's go, Ron!" she says. "We've got to find Falsetto!"

"Here I am, Kim Possible!" Falsetto squeals. "And I'm ready for a fight!"

Falsetto drops into a martial-arts crouch. Kim puts up her fists and keeps her eyes on the minicomputer.

While Kim gets ready to fight, the chamster unties her shoelaces. She trips and lands on her back, on the edge of the bridge.

Falsetto says, "So, Kim Possible. This is the end. Once I'm done with you, all I have to do is use the codes in this minicomputer"—he holds

Go to the next page.

it up for Kim to see—"and all the money in Global Bank will be mine!" He smiles. "So, do you have one last wish?"

"Yeah," says Kim. "Can I put on some lip gloss?"

Falsetto nods.

Kim unscrews the top, but instead of applying it, she presses a button, which sends a jet of sticky goo at the computer. With a jerk of her hand, Kim sends the computer flying into the East River.

"Noooooo!" cries Falsetto. Kim leaps up and uses her grappling hook to tie him up.

"Looks like your plan went to the dogs, Falsetto," Kim says.

👍 **You win! If you have captured all the villains, turn to page 52.**

👍 **To pick another villain, turn to page 6.**

Kim and Ron arrive at the TV producer's office building. As they ride the elevator to the thirty-fifth floor, Ron asks, "What are we going to say to this lady, Kim? Why do you think she knows where White Stripe is?"

Kim says, "We know White Stripe robbed the bank so he could make his own TV show, right? I'll bet she talked to White Stripe. She might even be in on the plan." The elevator stops and Kim and Ron walk into the offices of Joan Ferronikus Productions.

"Can I help you?" the receptionist asks.

"Uh . . . yes," says Kim. "We're looking for Ms. Ferronikus."

"She's not in," says the receptionist. "She is

Go to the next page.

on location for the next six months. Good-bye."

No TV producer means no White Stripe. But maybe there's a clue in her office!

"Say," says Kim. "Wasn't that Colin Frando I saw out in the hall? You know, the big movie star?" Kim elbows Ron.

"Why . . . yes, Kim, it was Colin."

The receptionist jumps up. "I love Colin. I have to get his autograph. Hey, kids," she calls over her shoulder. "Watch the door, will ya?"

Kim and Ron tiptoe into Ms. Ferronikus's office. It's huge. Suddenly the desk chair spins around. "Aaaaaaaa!" screams Ron.

"What my friend means to say," Kim began, "is that we're aaaabsolutely thrilled to meet you, ma'am. We were wondering if you were interested in White Stripe's new TV show."

"That has-been? I told him that no one in town would want to produce his show unless he got a lot of other funding together. I haven't heard from him since."

"Looks like the trail's gone cold, K.P.," Ron says.

👎 **You lose. But don't get tweaked—turn to page 75 and play again!**

"**W**haddya think, Ron? Paris sure is beautiful, eh?" says Kim.

But Ron doesn't reply.

Kim looks over at Ron. His face is frozen. "Ron?"

"Get. Me. Off. NOW!" shouts Ron. "Please, Kim? I think I'm going to be sick."

Kim looks down at her Club Banana hoodie. It's brand new. Does she really want to take a chance on Ron's delicate stomach? She could always go the rest of the way on her own.

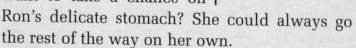

"Okay, Ron." Kim undoes her clamp and hops onto a beam, pulling Ron with her. "I'm going to keep going. You wait here."

Kim climbs for a few minutes. Just as she reaches the level with the bird's nest, Aviarius rises up, clutching bags of money. He spots Kim and cackles as he flies away.

👎 **You lose. To play again, turn to page 59.**

When Kim and Ron get to the bank, lines of angry people are waiting for tellers. The ATMs have signs reading COMPUTERS DOWN. The bank manager is running around looking frazzled.

Kim runs over to the manager. "What's going on?" she asks him.

"It's terrible! The computers are down and we can't open the safe—it's computerized, too! We're in big trouble!" wails the manager.

"How did this happen?" asks Kim.

"We got a huge online deposit, so big I couldn't even count the zeros. And just like that—pffft! Every last bit of data is gone. I don't even know how much money I have."

"I smell a rat—no, a skunk," Kim says to Ron.

"Yeah, too bad he got away," Ron says. "I don't think there's anything else we can do."

👎 **You lose—that stinks. But you can play again by turning to page 75.**

Downstairs Kim and Ron duck into the kitchen. Ron opens the fridge. All that's in it are a couple of cans of half-empty dog food. "Wow," says Ron. "Doesn't anybody in this house eat? The fridge is, like, totally empty."

"Are we getting warm, Wade?" Kim asks into the Kimmunicator.

"I'm not getting anything right now, Kim," Wade replies.

Kim thinks. There's no sign of Falsetto down here. Wade can't get a signal.

"Okay," says Kim. "Let's try upstairs." She and Ron turn around.

🌐 **Turn to page 14.**

"*T*hat was one crowded train, Kim!" says Ron as they walk up the steps at the Eiffel Tower station.

"It's called the Metro, Ron, and it wouldn't have been so bad if you hadn't given Rufus his own seat. I don't think the lady with five shopping bags was too happy," says Kim.

The tower is straight ahead. The lines to take the elevator to the top are very long. Kim debates using her special suction-cup shoes to climb up the side of the tower. But that means Ron will have to ride piggyback. What should Kim do?

🌐 **To take the elevator, turn to page 38.**

🌐 **To climb the side of the tower, turn to page 57.**

Kim grabs onto the ivy growing up the side of the house and climbs up. Ron follows. "Don't look down," calls Kim. From this height, Kim can see the East River and the Brooklyn Bridge. Boats are crisscrossing the water, and the sun feels warm on her face.

Cool! thinks Kim. I can catch some rays while I'm fighting crime!

On the second floor, Kim climbs to a window. It's locked. The house is very old, and the bricks beneath the ivy are soft and crumbly. Kim has to be careful not to put too much weight on one foot as she pushes and pulls her way up the side of the house.

"Ouch!" Ron calls, as bits of brick bounce off his face.

"Sorry, Ron!" calls Kim.

On the third floor Kim finds an open window. She wiggles it open with one hand and

Go to the next page.

squirms in. It's a bathroom. Ron drops to the floor and lies down. "Phew! I'm bushed!" he says with a sigh.

Wade comes in on the Kimmunicator. "Kim, that handheld computer is giving off a very strong signal and it's not far from you. Keep looking. I'll tell you if you're getting warmer."

Kim and Ron creep out into the hallway. "This house is huge," whispers Ron. "I wonder if there's a pool on the roof." Kim gives Ron a dirty look and they keep moving.

Should they look downstairs, look upstairs, or stay on this floor?

🌐 **To look upstairs, turn to page 14.**

🌐 **To stay on the same floor, turn to page 39.**

🌐 **To look downstairs, turn to page 46.**

Kim and Ron arrive at the legendary HOLLY-WOOD sign.

"I'll climb to the top and see if I can spot White Stripe," Kim says.

"This is much larger than it looks on TV, K.P.," Ron says, breathing hard as he struggles to keep up.

Kim pulls herself up to the horizontal bar of the "H" and spies White Stripe fifty feet above her, typing on his laptop. A couple of bags of cash are sitting next to him. He yells, "This online banking is not as easy as it looks!"

I guess he doesn't know that he has to take the money to the bank to deposit it, thinks Kim. I've got to stop him before he realizes.

Kim slips. She pulls herself up to the same level as White Stripe. Kim tiptoes up behind him, but he senses her presence and jumps up.

"Kim Possible!" he yells. "I should have known you'd try to stop me! Well, it won't work!" White Stripe lets loose a blast of stink spray that sends Kim to her knees, coughing.

When Kim is able to stand again, she sees that White Stripe is still typing on his laptop. She pulls out her compact/zip line and takes

Go to the next page.

aim. She hooks the cover of the laptop and jerks it back. The computer flies through the air and lands on the ground with a crash.

"Lucky for me, that is still under warranty, Kim Possible," White Stripe cries as he blasts some stink spray. Kim jumps and avoids it.

She throws an extrahard front kick, but White Stripe jumps out of the way. The force of Kim's kick spins her right off the sign! She grabs onto the edge of the sign, hanging on by her fingers. White Stripe walks over and peers down at her.

"Good-bye, Kim Possible," he says, as he pries her fingers loose.

🌐 To see what happens to Kim, turn to page 13.

"**W**oo-chow! What a day," says Ron as he flops onto the couch at Kim's house.

"Tell me something I don't know," Kim says as she brings a soda from the kitchen and sits down with Ron. "Paris, Los Angeles, New York, even right here in town—I can't believe we got all four villains in one day," says Kim.

Rufus chatters from Ron's pocket. "Rufus says, 'We're a good team!'" chuckles Ron.

"Yeah, we are," says Kim.

"I'm beat. I just want to sit here for a minute and—"

BEEP! BEEP! The Kimmunicator goes off.

"Looks like it's time for another mission," Kim says with a smile.

👍 **Congratulations! You helped Kim, Ron, and Rufus save the world.**

Kim and Ron dash over to the fire escape and start to climb down.

A minute later, they hear the dogs barking from the roof. They just made it!

Kim stops part of the way down and calls Wade. "What's the sitch?"

"I've got a very strong signal, Kim. I say keep going," Wade replies. "I'll tell you if you're getting warmer."

Kim and Ron run down the fire escape, looking in the windows for signs of Falsetto. They see the snarling dogs running back downstairs.

Turn to the next page.

"Faster, K.P., faster. Let's get out of here," Ron says.

When they get down to the street, it looks deserted.

"Warmer," says Wade. "Definitely warmer." Kim and Ron walk faster, looking all around.

"Falsetto is here somewhere," whispers Ron. "I can feel it!"

"Way warmer!" calls Wade.

They enter the park. Little kids are running around playing tag. A couple of mothers are pushing strollers. But where is Falsetto?

Then they see someone on a park bench, huddled over a minicomputer.

"That's got to be him!" says Kim. They dash over. Kim sneaks up behind him and snatches the minicomputer.

"Hey! Give me back my computer!" shouts a teenage boy. He walks over to Kim and retrieves his computer as she stares in shock. "I'm IMing my girlfriend. And it's private!"

👎 **You lost Falsetto. Turn to page 15 to play again.**

Kim decides to see if the tellers know anything. "Hey, wake up!" she shouts. A woozy teller rubs his eyes and sits up.

"Peeee-eww!" he says. "Oh, my head."

Kim asks the teller what happened. He says that a man wearing a Bueno Nacho uniform came into the bank and blasted the place with a smelly spray. The next thing the teller knew, Kim was shaking him awake.

Ron walks over to Kim and says, "I found a deposit slip for another bank. And it's got White Stripe's name on it! We've got to go there!"

The teller says, "But what about the guy in the Bueno Nacho uniform? He's the one who did this!"

"Bueno Nacho! Oh, Kim, if White Stripe is besmirching the good name of the Nacho, we've got to stop him!

Should Kim go to the other bank or look for White Stripe at the nearest Bueno Nacho?

🌐 **To go to the other bank, turn to page 23.**

🌐 **To go to Bueno Nacho, turn to page 67.**

*I*n the T-shirt aisle, Kim spots Bonnie talking on her cell.

"Mother, I am *so* not going to spend a lot of money on his birthday present. I don't care if he's my only brother!" She holds the phone away from her ear as a voice on the other end squawks loudly. "*Whatever!*" Bonnie snaps the phone shut.

Bonnie looks around to make sure no one she knows is watching and holds a T-shirt up against herself to see if it's the right size.

Well, that's definitely not for her brother, Kim thinks. It looks like Bonnie actually buys clothes for herself at Smarty Mart.

Even though it'd be fun to bust Bonnie, Kim is *so* not in the mood to deal with her right now.

What should Kim do?

🌐 **To search for the biker, turn to page 21.**

🌐 **To stay with Bonnie, turn to page 24.**

🌐 **To look for the old lady, turn to page 70.**

*S*mack-thwock! *Smack-thwock!* Kim's shoes make a funny sound as she rappels her way up the tower. Ron clings to her as they ascend. "Don't look down, Ron!" yells Kim.

Kim can see the giant nest above her. She stops on a crossbeam.

"Phew, Kim!" says Ron. "That was a good workout!"

"Shh!" says Kim as they tiptoe to the nest.

A noise comes from inside the nest. Kim jumps into the nest, ready to attack . . . and lands next to a very frightened pigeon eating the remnants of a hot dog roll. Dozens of pigeons swarm over to help their feathered friend.

Kim sees a single coin in the nest. It's too late. Aviarius is long gone.

☞ **You lost Aviarius. To try to catch him again, turn to page 59.**

After depositing a very unhappy Ron on a gargoyle, Kim flies all the way to the top of the tower. She glides in through a large, open window and lands on the stone floor. The inside of the tower is dark. Kim fumbles for her glitter pen/halogen searchlight.

There's a funny squeaking sound. And it's getting closer. What's that noise? Kim thinks.

The noise gets louder and louder. Kim keeps  digging around for the light. Where is it? she thinks. Finally, her hand touches the searchlight. She whips it out and flips the "on" switch. Aviarius's army of heat-seeking hummingbirds is flying right at her!

Kim ducks, covering her head with her hands. She points the beam from the super-strong, superhot light out the window. The hummingbirds follow the hot light—right out of the tower! Kim is safe!

🌐 **Turn to page 73.**

"**I** can't believe how beautiful Paris is, Ron!" says Kim as they walk near the Seine River.

"I can't believe how many tourists there are!" Ron replies. "Some guy just stepped on my toes. Yeesh! Time for some food." Ron walks toward a street vendor who's selling crepes.

"Hmm," Ron says. "They look like pancakes, but thinner. And I don't see any maple syrup. Don't you have any French fries or French toast?"

Meanwhile, Kim spots a newspaper and translates the headline: GLOBAL BANK ROBBED! She calls Wade.

"Wade here," comes a voice over her Kimmunicator. The picture kicks in to show Wade with a croissant. "Since you're in France, I thought I'd eat something French."

Turn to the next page.

"Wade, we're too late. Aviarius already robbed the bank!" Kim scans the article for clues. "I can't believe he did it so fast!"

Wade punches some keys and then whistles. "Wow, Kim. He really got away with a lot!"

Ron walks over with a crepe. "He took a big heaping pile o' money, did he? Enough to really feather his nest?" Rufus giggled. "Get it, Kim? *Feather* his nest? 'Cause he's a bird, sort of."

Kim gets it. "Okay, Ron. We've got to start looking for . . . hey, what's this?" Kim sees a small article near the bottom of the front page.

It's about two enormous birds' nests that

appeared mysteriously in the Cathedral of Notre Dame and the Eiffel Tower.

"I think we know where to start looking for Aviarius, Wade! Who else would build gigantic birds' nests?"

"But which place should we try first, Kim?" asks Ron. "Notre Dame is the big old

Go to the next page.

cathedral with all those spooky gargoyles, right? And the Eiffel Tower—doesn't that have a restaurant in it? It's going to be dinnertime in a couple of hours!"

Wade says, "You'd better get going. Aviarius won't keep that money in his nests for very long, and once it's gone—it's gone!"

Should Kim and Ron investigate the nest at the Cathedral of Notre Dame? Or the one at the Eiffel Tower? It's time for you to help out!

🌐 **To go to Notre Dame, turn to page 12.**

🌐 **To go to the Eiffel Tower, turn to page 47.**

Ron and Kim stop at the entrance to the alley. It's dark, and they can't see much. They hear a rustling noise and turn around. A cat walks out from under some garbage. "Phew," says Ron. "I thought it was the chamster." Kim moves into the alley. Ron follows her, and Rufus takes up the rear.

Kim can barely make out something up ahead. She turns to Ron and says, "Shh," putting a finger to her lips. She backs up against the wall and tiptoes forward, pulling her Ninja star/blush case out of her purse. She moves closer and closer. Finally, she comes to the end of the alley. Where is Falsetto Jones?

Kim turns to Ron, but before she can speak, she hears a squeak from above. Falsetto Jones is on the fire escape!

Falsetto leaps down onto Kim. They tumble to the ground. Falsetto slaps Kim.

"Ouch!" Kim yells. "When was the last time you cut your fingernails?"

Kim lands one good

62

Go to the next page.

punch to Falsetto's head, but his hair gel makes her fist slip off. "Ha!" snickers Falsetto.

Kim backs up for a side kick, but Falsetto turns and starts to run. Kim pulls her ninja star from its case and lets it fly. *Ziing!* The star catches part of Falsetto's ruffly shirt and pins it to the wall, but Falsetto breaks free. He looks at his designer shirt and glares at Kim before breaking into a run.

Over his shoulder, Falsetto calls, "This is an expensive shirt, Kim Possible! You'll pay for this!"

Kim and Ron follow him. At the corner they see him slip in the side door of an enormous old house that juts out over the East River.

"C'mon, Ron," says Kim. "It's time to show that guy he's barking up the wrong tree."

🌐 **Turn to page 48.**

Kim and Ron look around. No White Stripe. But the door to the street is open.

Kim leaps through the doorway and lands in a Ninja strike pose on the side-walk outside.

"Waaaaaah!" screams a little boy who's playing on the sidewalk.

"Aaaaaaaah!" screams Ron, who drops to the ground and covers his face.

"Oh, brother," says Kim. She looks around. White Stripe's Bueno Nacho uniform is on the ground. In the pocket is a TV producer's business card. She also notices a fresh tire tread. It looks like one of the delivery mopeds is gone. Should Kim visit the TV producer or take one of the other mopeds and look for White Stripe?

⊕ To visit the TV producer, turn to page 42.

⊕ To look for White Stripe on the moped, turn to page 72.